Police TV

Tim Vicary

Illustrated by
Dylan Teague

OXFORD
UNIVERSITY PRESS

OXFORD
UNIVERSITY PRESS

Great Clarendon Street, Oxford OX2 6DP

Oxford University Press is a department of the University of Oxford.
It furthers the University's objective of excellence in research, scholarship,
and education by publishing worldwide in

Oxford New York

Auckland Cape Town Dar es Salaam Hong Kong Karachi
Kuala Lumpur Madrid Melbourne Mexico City Nairobi
New Delhi Shanghai Taipei Toronto

With offices in

Argentina Austria Brazil Chile Czech Republic France Greece
Guatemala Hungary Italy Japan Poland Portugal Singapore
South Korea Switzerland Thailand Turkey Ukraine Vietnam

OXFORD and OXFORD ENGLISH are registered trade marks of
Oxford University Press in the UK and in certain other countries

ISBN-13: 978 0 19 423171 8
ISBN-10: 0 19 423171 2

Printed in Hong Kong

Illustrated by: Dylan Teague

Oxford Bookworms Starters

(250 headwords)

Original fiction for students starting to read in
English. Stories are carefully graded and supported
by clear, high-quality illustrations.

Oxford Bookworms Library

A wide range of original and adapted stories, both
classic and modern, which take learners from
elementary to advanced level through six carefully
graded language stages.

Oxford Bookworms Playscripts

A range of plays, designed both for reading and
performing in the classroom.

Oxford Bookworms Factfiles

Original readers giving varied and interesting
information about a range of non-fiction topics.

Oxford Bookworms Collection

Fiction by well-known classic and modern authors.
Texts are not abridged or simplified in any way.

1 THE JOGGER

Dan and Sue are police officers in London. It is a Tuesday morning, and Dan is angry.

'What's the matter, Dan?' Sue asks.

'Look at this,' Dan says. 'Every day someone steals money from people near the shops. We must stop this.'

'Yes, of course,' Sue says. 'But who is it?'

'There is a jogger,' Dan says. 'Every day he runs near the shops. Sometimes he runs into people. Perhaps he steals the money.'

'OK,' Sue says. 'Let's go to the shops. Perhaps we can see this jogger.'

They sit upstairs in a window over the shops. Dan has a radio. They watch the people in the street.

'Look!' Sue says. 'There's the jogger!'

The young man runs into an old woman, and she falls down. The jogger puts his hand on the old woman's arm. 'I'm sorry,' he says. 'Can I help you? Here's your bag.'

Then a young woman shouts at him. 'Don't run here!' she says. 'It's dangerous! Go away!'

The young man runs away. Dan talks in his radio. 'Quick! Stop him! He's running up North Street!'

A police car stops the young man in North Street.

'Are you OK now?' Sue asks the old woman.

'Yes, thank you. Where is that nice young woman? I can't see her now.'

'Have you got all your money?' Sue asks.

The old woman looks in her bag. 'No, I haven't! My money's in my purse. But my purse isn't here!'

'OK Sue,' Dan says. 'Let's talk to the jogger!'

'Who are you?' Sue asks the young man.

'My name's Peter Jones. Why? Who are you?'

'We're police officers. Why do you go running past the shops every day?'

'Why not? I like running.'

'OK,' Dan says. 'Let's look for the money.'

'What money?' Peter Jones asks. 'What are you talking about? I never take money with me when I run.'

Dan looks for the money but he cannot find any.

'Can I go now?' Peter Jones asks.

'OK,' Dan says angrily. 'But don't come back!'

'Why not?' Peter asks angrily. 'I live here! And I'm not doing anything wrong!' He runs away.

'What do we do now?' Sue asks. 'Where is the old woman's money, and her purse?'

'I don't know,' says Dan. 'Somebody has it. But who?'

2 TV

Dan and Sue go back to the shops. 'I don't understand,' Dan says. 'The jogger hasn't got the money so we must look for someone different.'

'Look,' Sue says. 'There's a TV camera over that shop door. Perhaps that can help us.'

They go into the shop and watch the video.

'Look,' Sue says. 'There's the old woman. She's getting money from the bank and putting it into her purse. Now she's putting the purse into the bag.'

'Stop the video there,' says Dan. 'Now, look carefully. Is anybody watching her?'

'There are a lot of people in the street,' Sue says. 'I'm not sure. Is it that man with the long hair?'

CAM:1
10:15 am

'Perhaps,' says Dan. 'Let's go on. What happens next?'

They watch the video. The jogger runs into the old lady. He stops and helps her. She shouts at him and he runs away. Then a lot of people come and help the old lady.

'Look!' Sue says. 'The long-haired man has her arm.'

'Yes, but that woman has her bag,' Dan says. 'What's she doing with it? Oh! I can't see! There's a man in front of her!'

'Listen, I have an idea,' Dan says. 'You go to the bank tomorrow, and take some money out.'

'Why's that a good idea?' Sue asks.

'Because we can watch you,' Dan answers. 'Get a lot of money from the bank, and let everybody in the street see it. Take a radio too, so you can talk to me.'

'OK,' Sue says. 'We can do that tomorrow morning, then.'

❸ HELP ME! QUICK!

Next day Sue goes to the bank. Dan is watching with another policeman, Jim. They have radios.

'I'm getting the money now,' Sue says.

'That's good, Sue,' Dan says on his radio. 'Now let everybody see it.'

Sue drops some money near her feet. People in the street look at her.

'Look – there's the man with the long hair!' Jim says. 'He's picking up the money. Shall I arrest him?'

'No, wait,' Dan says. 'Watch.'

The man picks up the money and gives it to Sue. 'Here you are,' he says. 'That's a lot of money – be careful!'

'Thanks,' Sue says.

'That's OK.' The man smiles and walks away.

'Have you got all the money, Sue?' Dan asks by radio. 'Yes, it's all here,' Sue says. 'What can I do now?'

'Buy some things in the shops, and then walk slowly down the street,' Dan says. 'We're watching you.'

Sue buys some apples, milk and bread. Then she walks slowly down the street. Dan and Jim watch her go.

'Is anybody following me?' Sue asks.

'No,' Dan says. 'There's a woman with a baby. That's all.'

'Don't follow me,' Sue says into the radio. 'Nobody must see you. I'm turning right, into Smith Street . . . now I'm turning left into Peg Lane. The woman with the baby is following me . . . I'm turning right, into Dale Avenue.'

'Are there lots of people about?' Dan asks.

'No, it's very quiet. Nothing is happening.'

Dan and Jim wait. Then Sue shouts: 'Be careful! Oh, help me, quick! Help!'

The jogger, Peter Jones, runs into Sue and she falls over. There are apples, milk and bread everywhere.

'I'm sorry,' says the man. 'Let me help you.'

The woman takes Sue's arm. 'Are you OK?' she asks. 'Go away!' she shouts at the man.

But he sees the radio in Sue's pocket. 'What's this?' he asks. 'A police radio? Give me the money, quick!'

He takes the money and runs.

The woman wants to run after him but Sue holds her. 'Stop!' she says. 'I'm a police officer. You must stay here!'

'But why?' the woman asks. 'I want to help you. That man has your money – I haven't got it!'

'Is he your friend?' Sue asks. 'Where does he live?'

'I don't know,' the woman says. 'I don't know him.'

'Who are you?' Sue asks. 'Where do you live?'

'Linda . . . Linda Wilks. I live at 14, Old Street.'

4 MAN WITH A KNIFE

Dan runs up to Sue. 'Are you OK?' he asks.

'Yes, I'm OK,' she says. 'Go on, Dan – run!'

Sue calls a police car on her radio. Dan runs after Peter Jones. 'Jim, he's turning left into Dock Lane!' he shouts. 'Can you see him?'

'I can see him but he's running very fast,' Jim says. The jogger sees Jim and gets into a boat. Jim runs to the river and gets into the boat, too.

'Stop!' Jim says. 'I'm a police officer – Oh no!'

The jogger, Peter Jones, hits Jim and he falls into the water. The boat goes across the river.

Dan helps Jim out of the water. 'He's going into a café,' Dan says. 'Come on – let's run to that bridge!'

They go across the bridge and run to the café. Jim goes behind the café and Dan goes in.

'Is he in there?' Jim asks on his radio.

'Yes,' Dan answers. 'Jim – he's coming out!'

'Stop,' says Jim. 'I'm a police officer.'

But Peter has a knife in his hand.

Jim holds out his hand. 'Give me the knife, Peter.'

'Stay back!' Peter says. 'I can kill you with this.'

Jim can see Dan in the door behind Peter. Dan walks out of the door, very slowly and quietly.

'Come on, Peter,' says Jim. 'Give me the knife.'

Dan takes Peter's arms from behind, and Jim takes the knife from his hand. Dan finds the money in Peter's trousers.

5 AT THE POLICE STATION

'I want to go home now,' says Linda. 'My baby is hungry and tired.'

'Do you know Peter Jones?' Sue asks. 'Do you and Peter steal money from people?'

'No, I don't know him. And I never steal money.'

'Do you know this woman, Peter?' Dan asks.

'No,' says Peter. 'I don't know her. Who is she?'

Dan and Sue go back to their office.

'Does Linda work with Peter?' Dan asks Sue.

'Yes, she does,' says Sue. 'Watch this video. Look – there she is! She's watching me get the money, and now she's talking to someone on her phone.'

'But who is she talking to?'

'She's talking to Peter, of course. Now she's following me and talking to him again. She's talking about me.'

Dan and Sue speak to Linda again.

'Can I see your phone, please, Ms Wilks?' Sue asks.

'My phone? Why do you want to see that?'

'Well, it remembers a lot of numbers.'

Sue presses *1* on Linda's phone. Peter's phone begins to ring. Sue laughs. 'Let me ask you again, Ms Wilks. Do you know Peter Jones?'

'Well, yes, OK. I know him. But I don't steal money.'

Sue and Dan take Linda home. They go into her house.

'There's two hundred pounds under your bed, Linda,' Dan says. 'And look – this is the old lady's purse.'

'This is a nice photo of you and the baby,' Sue says. 'But who is the man? Is he the baby's father?'

'OK, it's Peter,' says Linda. 'And yes, I do steal the money. I'm sorry, OK?'

'No, Linda, it's not OK,' Sue says. 'It's not OK at all.'

Before Reading

1 Look at the front and back covers and then answer the questions. Tick one box for each question.

1 When does the story happen?
   a ☐ In the present.
   b ☐ In the future.
   c ☐ Long ago.

2 Who is the story about?
   a ☐ Young people.
   b ☐ Older people.
   c ☐ Children.

3 Who are the people in the picture?
   a ☐ Friends.
   b ☐ Strangers.
   c ☐ Relatives.

4 What does the story make you feel?
   a ☐ Frightened.
   b ☐ Excited.
   c ☐ .... (You can write your own answer.)

While Reading

1 Read pages 1–3 and then answer these questions.

1 What happens every day near the shops?
   a ☐ A woman likes running there.
   b ☐ Someone takes money from people.
   c ☐ Dan and Sue go shopping

2 What does the young man do to the old woman?
   a ☐ He puts his hand on her arm.
   b ☐ He puts his hand on her leg.
   c ☐ He takes her bag

2 Read pages 4–6. Who says this in the story?

1 'Have you got all your money?'
2 'My purse isn't here!
3 'I like running.'
4 'OK. But don't come back!'

3 Read Chapter 2. Answer these questions.

1 What does Sue see over the shop door?
2 What do Dan and Sue do in the shop?
3 How many people come to help the old lady?
4 Who goes to the bank and takes some money out?

4 Read Chapter 3.
Are these statements true (T) or false (F)?

	T	F
1 The man with the long hair picks up the money.	☐	☐
2 The man with the long hair takes the money from Sue.	☐	☐
3 Sue is following a woman with a baby.	☐	☐
4 It's very quiet in Dale Avenue.	☐	☐
5 Peter Jones takes the radio from Sue's pocket.	☐	☐

5 Read Chapter 4. Answer these questions.

Who

1 . . . calls a police car on her radio?

2 . . . hits Jim?

3 . . . helps Jim out of the water?

4 . . . goes behind the cafe?

5 . . . takes Peter's arms from behind?

6 Before you read Chapter 5,
can you guess what happens?

	YES	NO
1 The police take Peter to the police station.	☐	☐
2 Linda knows Peter.	☐	☐
3 Linda tries to help Peter.	☐	☐
4 Linda is angry with Peter.	☐	☐
5 Peter runs away, but Linda finds him.	☐	☐

After Reading

1 Use these words to join these sentences together.

and   but   so   because

1 Peter Jones runs into the old woman. She falls down.
2 The old woman looks in her bag. She can't find her purse.
3 Dan has a radio. He can talk to Sue.
4 Peter is afraid. He sees a radio in Sue's pocket.

2 Put these seven sentences in the right order.

a ☐ Peter Jones runs into Sue.
b ☐ She drops the money in the street.
c ☐ Sue walks into Smith Street, Peg Lane, and Dale Avenue.
d ☐ He sees the radio in her pocket, takes her money, and runs.
e ☐ The blue-haired man picks up the money and gives it to her.
f ☐ The woman with the baby follows her.
g ☐ Sue takes some money out of the bank.

3 Look at each picture, then answer the questions after it.

1    Who is this?
            What is she doing?

2    Who is this?
            What is she doing?

3    Who is this?
            What is she doing?

4    Who is this?
            Who is she talking to?

5    Who is this?
            What is he doing?

6    Who is this?
            What is he doing?

Glossary

arrest (*vb*) when the police find a bad man and take him to the police station

bridge a road or path that goes over water

buy get something from a shop with money

café a place where you sit and drink coffee or tea

dangerous something that can hurt you is dangerous

follow walk behind someone

idea something you think

jogger a runner

let make it easy for something to happen

officer a man or woman in the police

purse a small bag for money

shout talk very loudly

steal take something that is not yours

turn go left or right